THE PROFESSOR WAS
DEAD

THE PROFESSOR WAS

DEAD

6/16/22

Anthony J. Agostinelli
125 Quaker Hill Lane
Suite 204
Portsmouth RI 02871-4073
ajagostinelli@gmail.com
401-480-5397

For you Robin —
My dancing
friend Tony

Anthony J Agostinelli

ANTHONY J. AGOSTINELLI

Library of Congress Control Number: 2013909491
ISBN: Hardcover   978-1-4836-4473-8
                 Softcover   978-1-4836-4472-1
                 Ebook   978-1-4836-4474-5

Rev. date: 05/24/2013

To order additional copies of this book, contact:
Xlibris Corporation
1-888-795-4274
www.Xlibris.com
Orders@Xlibris.com
135458

Other Works and Monographs by
Anthony J. Agostinelli

- **The Wrath of Grapes, 1973**
- All Jazz Is Fusion, 1986
- Eddie Safranzki: A Retrospective, 1992
- Don Ellis: A Man for Our Time, 1984
- How to Do Jazz Research, 1987
- The Newport Jazz Festival, Rhode Island (1954-1971): A Significant Era in the Development of Jazz, 1978
- The Newport Jazz Festival, Rhode Island (1954-1971): A Bibliography, Discography and Filmography, 1978
- The Professor Was Dead, 2009
- Some Rhode Island Jazz Notables, 1984
- Stan Kenton: The Many Musical Moods of His Orchestras, 6th Printing, 1999; © 1985
- Urban Contemporary Jazz, 1988
- **The Claudia Stories, 2014-2018**

Dedication

For Barbara, whose persistence to live
brings me great joy!

Acknowledgements:

We do not create written works on our own. There are those within our lives who by their own presence – living and dead -- have helped to shape our world-view. All is from God. I acknowledge these people who influenced me: my wife Barbara, who supported me in every one of many endeavors, who even now, supports and cares for those around her; my grandfather Antonio, who was a great story teller, reader of books and poetry; my grandmother Irena, who fed and watched over; my grandmother, Maria Giuseppe, who showed me love – and a broom swing at me when I would tease her; my father Domenic, who provided me with direction to love and help my neighbor; my mother Louise, who did what mothers should do – nurture me; some of my academic, music and life mentors: Lorenzo "D'Ag" D'Agostino, SSE; Sisters Mary Ellen, and Catherine of the Assumption, SND; Vin D'Alessio; Jack McCall, SJ; my special long-standing friends with whom Barbara and I shared our lives; and those new friends among whom I live. My children, their spouses and their children, who show me great respect and support.

Thanks go to the Xlibris team who has made this manuscript publishable.

Anthony J. Agostinelli
May 19, 2013

PROLOGUE

It was sunset time. In a short while, the sky would turn sky-blue pink as the earth turned away from the sun and the clouds remained. Professor Anthony J. L'Alba ("AJ" to his students, colleagues, friends, and the John Adams College community) looked out from his study window, at the Wolfen Manse as the orange red sun disappeared to the south west of Wolfen Lake, Massachusetts. For a few moments, the cross atop the church of St. Gregory the Great at the monastery after the same name was mirrored in the center of the late spring ginger sun. He had watched sunsets for over 40 years from his study, a study that announced, 'An old college professor confers here with his muse'. In spite of the tragedy, which occurred at the Manse some 50 years ago, AJ loved what had become his home[1]. His study was replete with bookcases of burnished oak, a great old desk with matching chair and a grandfather's clock, other odd pieces—a veritable cornucopia of artifacts belonging to a tenured professor. A 1955 graduate of John Adams College, AJ had been hired in the early 1960s as an instructor of History after he had completed his studies at Harvard University. He received a Master of Arts in History/Philosophy in 1959 (MA).

One of his Benedictine monk mentors, Dom Damian Wilson, suggested that AJ study a year or two at the Pontifical North American

---

[1]   AJ signed a letter of agreement that he was to be sole tenant of Wolfen Manse for as long as he remained as member of the faculty of John Adams College. He did consider the Manse as his "home."

College in Rome to deepen his knowledge of philosophy and theology. Damian recommended his admission and AJ stayed on and graduated with multiple degrees—history, philosophy and theology; he met many priests who were educated like himself in the sun's rays of the Vatican, which gave him a certain status amongst priests and others in the Roman Catholic Church. There, he became friends with a many priests who would go on and become bishops, archbishops, and cardinals. In particular, he became a close friend with a priest, Monsignor Aldo Ciminiano who would eventually become a cardinal then Pope Andrew; AJ was given the Cross for the Church and Pontiff, or *Cross Pro Ecclesia et Pontifice,* which is "bestowed on persons, both laypersons and clergy, who have given service to the Church." Because of a particularly sensitive theological issue, Pope Andrew appointed AJ a "lay cardinal" after suspending the ban against this practice, because of the extraordinary nature of his service to the Church . . . but that is part of another story.

He finally won his Doctor of History (Ph.D.) (1966). AJ was a trained classical pianist. One of the monks at the Abbey (Dom Filippo Ansino) played the world concert stage as a prominent pianist before he entered the monastery at St. Gregory's, and took AJ on as a pupil. AJ was very much exposed to the world of music—orchestral, chamber music, opera, Broadway musicals and jazz. He was highly influenced by the music of the progressive jazz artists, notably Stan Kenton. Like Andre Previn, his contemporary, he also played jazz.

He had risen in rank to Professor of History in the Wolfen Family Chair. In addition to his many historical works, which dealt with crimes over the years since the dawn of recorded history, he had also grown in fame as an amateur sleuth among his colleagues. He had solved crimes in the Wolfen area and elsewhere. His fame as a sleuth was known everywhere. The Roman Catholic Church and many organizations and corporations called upon AJ to investigate quietly mysterious and criminal activity within those very institutions (See notes following: "Pope Andrew Abdicates")

He was about 70 years of age. Because of his devotion to study, regular exercise, a healthy diet, and a spiritual regimen (which had begun when he was in the elementary grades) which included daily Mass at the Abbey of St. Gregory the Great [on the southwestern side of Lake Wolfen] and to the prolific writing of mystery novels, he looked younger than his [chronological] years. He was slim, just around six feet tall, with salt and pepper hair, a prominent nose, which at the was center of his Tuscanesque face. He was dressed in formal attire in preparation for a formal dinner that was about to be held at the College. He was known amongst the college and town as distinguished and handsome!

AJ grew up at the Monastery. He was an only child. The Monks employed his parents—his father Domenico ("Minicucce"[2] was his nickname), was the head grounds keeper and his mother Maria Luigia, and was the principal cook for the monks. They lived in the gatehouse of the Abbey—his parents from the 1920s, and he, from his birth in 1933. His parents' ancestors came from Alba in Italy; their family name was Albarone. Upon arrival at Boston in the late 1800s, the immigration officials confused the name of the family with the name of the town in Piedmont—Alba was the town, and Albarone was the family name. Therefore, the name went into the records as, "L'Alba," from Alba. The family kept the name, "L'Alba."

The English Benedictine monks, whose commitment to education of the young is well known, educated him. The Abbey school was primarily a residential school for the wealthy children of Roman Catholic families from all over the world, with a handful of day students. Just prior to World War II, many leading families from England sent their children to study and board at the Abbey school; as children were moved out of the major cities to the country, many were sent to the USA. The handfuls of children of parents who lived and worked at the Abbey were given a tuition-free education. After his parents died in the early 1950s, he continued to attend daily Mass at the Abbey, even while he was a student at Adams. He would run or bicycle the mile or so to the Abbey from the college. The groundskeeper's cottage was given over to Domenico's younger brother, Nicholas and his wife, Antonetta, who took over the

---

2   "Minicucc'" translates to "thousand heads" in dialect, although it means "hard head."

same duties as AJ's parents. AJ always had a place at the cottage until his uncle and aunt passed away in the late 1960s.

AJ always was aware of the time of day, since the Abbey always announced the monastic hours with a series of ringing bells. The tolling of the bells was also heard before the conventual Mass; in the latter instance, the bells were rung fifteen minutes before Mass; five minutes before Mass, and as the Monks assembled in the sanctuary, a continuous tolling of the bells was heard. He was seldom late for Mass, and instinctively knew the time of day without looking at his watch. Depending on which way the wind was blowing, the sound of the bells reached his ears at various volumes (depending on the wind direction and atmospheric conditions). The sounds of the bells were imbedded in his mind as part of his life's daily sounds.

———————————•—•———————————

It was almost 50 years that he and his life long friend, Deidre "DiDi" Ebersberger[3] had reported the events in conjunction with the death of Professor Richard Kurt Greenwood, who died in the very house in which AJ had lived since his hiring by President C. B. Wolfen in the early 1960s. AJ was a senior at John Adams College, and editor of the college newspaper at the time of Greenwood's death. DiDi was also a senior at the time and was the paper's star reporter.

DiDi and AJ were not considered an "item" at Adams. Since they had been friends and classmates during their days at the Abbey, their relationship was more like that of good friends or brother and sister, than anything else. Although there was a time when they approached their

---

[3] DiDi was also educated at the Abbey School. DiDi's father believed that the Monks would give her a more "classical" education than the local public school. She learned to play French horn, played in the school played in the school and college orchestra, and eventually played horn in the Pioneer Valley Orchestra, not too far from the town. She studied at Radcliffe College in Cambridge, and obtained her advanced degrees at Harvard University. In fact, many of the early families of Wolfen sent their children to the Abbey school for similar reasons.

teens, and later in their lives, they confided in each other about others whom caught their eye. Their deep friendship evolved because of their common interests—together they went hiking, camping, swimming, cross-country skiing, sailing on the lake, attended concerts at Boston's Symphony Hall, and at Tanglewood in Lenox, Massachusetts, played and listened to music, studied together,—two friends, who never entertained any other kind of relationship. Their strong friendship, their devotion to academic pursuits, and those things which they shared in common, were sufficient to their own personal lives, to not seek other close relationships. Over the years, they would also enjoy meals together with their parents—Italian-American and German-American meals from the "old country" became like "mother's milk" to them.

The Wolfen Manse was offered AJ when he was appointed instructor, because few in the college community wanted to live in this "house of death" as it became known after Greenwood's demise. The death of Greenwood shocked the town and College community. But after a short while, it was forgotten. Except Greenwood's death was not forgotten by AJ and DiDi. For AJ, Greenwood's demise was one of the few deaths that he could not logically explain. Such was the nature of the Greenwood's death in this small town in the Commonwealth of Massachusetts. AJ had a premonition that events surrounding Greenwood's death would emerge somehow this evening.

AJ and DiDi, were to attend the dinner for Honorary Degree candidates selected for the college's commencement. He could not dawdle much longer, since DiDi was to come for him, on her way to the home of the President. AJ did not tarry, and yet something in his mind was not right. Something was yet unfinished in what AJ always referred to as "the myth of the death of Richard Kurt Greenwood."

AJ was listening to a Stan Kenton composition "Theme to the West," on his newly purchased Bose radio/CD player, as he waited and watched the sunset.

CHAPTER ONE

The professor's head and shoulders were in the open gas oven in the kitchen of Wolfen House, where he lived in this rustic lakefront home. He was naked except for his white "balloon" under shorts. The grid metal shelves had been removed from the oven to give more room for his upper body to be thrust as far in as possible. He apparently had been lying there for some time when Greta Worley the woman who cleaned, and occasionally cooked for him, came to the house that morning. She detected the slight smell of gas in the air as she tried to open the kitchen door leading in from back porch. She had to push quite hard in order to break the seal of the black tape that had been used to seal the porch door. The smell of propane gas smell forced her to turn away. With the door partially opened, she could see the lower half of his body, legs akimbo, resting on the floor. Before she could do anything, Alvin Grabau came with a delivery of milk just at that time, and seeing what had transpired, elbowed his way past Greta and pushed his way into the kitchen with his elbow bent around his nose and face, to keep from breathing in the gas. The gas jet for the oven was turned on, which Alvin quickly turned off. He threw open the two windows over the sink, ripped the rest of the black tape off the porch door. He ran out to the porch to breathe. He ran back into the kitchen, coughing as he went, going to the kitchen door that led to the rest of the house, stripping off the tape, ran to the front of the house through the hallway, throwing open the front door. He ran back to the kitchen and found Greta hovering over the professor, repeating:

"The professor is dead! The professor is dead! The professor is dead!"

Alvin led Greta to the back porch, and sat her down on the back stairs. He went around to the front, ran up the front stairs, and into the hallway, where the downstairs phone was, and picked up the phone. By this time, the breeze off the lake had dissipated most of the lingering odor of gas. The local operator came on the line and in that distinctive New England small town voice, said:

"Good morning, Professor Greenwood, how may I help you?"

"This is Alvin, Tilly. Get me Sheriff Blocker, and hurry?"

"What's going on Alvin?" She recognized Alvin's voice. "Is the professor alright?"

"No time to talk now, Tilly, call the sheriff and send him out to Professor Greenwood's house right away. The professor is dead!"

"Oh my God! I'll get him right away!" Tilly Loehe knew how the town was run, another descendent from earliest settlers. She prided herself in knowing what went on because she was the operator for the local phone service; at the same time she did not indulge in gossiping about what she knew or found out from listening in on phone calls.

The steady breeze coming off Wolfen Lake, which was a stone's throw back of Greenwood's house, had blown most of the smell of propane gas away, and replaced it with the lake's own indefinable smell. Alvin went back down the hall, to the kitchen, to calm Greta.

Greta was back in the kitchen bent over Greenwood, mumbling something that Alvin could not understand. He looked over the scene. He quickly noticed then that the heavy-duty tape roll was lying on the floor within the reach of Greenwood's right hand. He again led her out to the porch.

"Greta," Alvin said, "you must stay out of there. It is too much for you to be in there with the Professor. You will make yourself sick. The Sheriff is coming. He'll know what to do."

Professor Richard Kurt Greenwood, aged 30, died in this month of May 1955, had been a popular professor of history at John Adams College in this quiet college town of Wolfen, Massachusetts.

An almost naked popular professor, dead, with his head and shoulders in the gas oven in his kitchen—this was a most bizarre event in the annals of this august institution of higher learning. It seemed like suicide, but was it?

CHAPTER TWO

John Adams is a small sectarian college in the town of Wolfen, Massachusetts on Lake Wolfen. Charles B. "CB" Wolfen Adams' tenth President, hired Greenwood, just after the end of World War II, upon recommendation of U.S. officials at Wittenberg, Germany, where Greenwood was a faculty member at the University of Wittenberg during and just after the war. After the war, the United States Government of Occupation in Germany was recommending many Germans to come to the United States, to make their lives here after a brutal war in Europe. Greenwood had been particularly helpful as a translator to the occupying forces. He also came highly recommended by the then U.S. Senator from Massachusetts.

CB was one of a long line of Wolfens who had led the college. Adams College was founded in 1861 by a coalition of Lutherans, who were settlers from Wittenberg, Germany, en route to Pennsylvania, in the early 1800s. Their ship docked at Boston for repairs. After some discussions, as the ship's repairs were taking longer than anticipated, they decided to leave the ship with their young families and all of their belongings to set out of Boston, via the trails out of Boston, heading westward. They purchased mules, wagons cattle and supplies; they set out along the road that is now Route 2 and along the Indian Path—the "Mohawk Trail." Transportation was extremely slow and roads were little more than wide paths cut through the wooded areas, supporting only foot, horse, and small carriage traffic. These roads tended to follow the "upper ground" in order to be self-draining. Consequently, the roads tended to be winding.

They journeyed through virgin timberlands, running brooks, broad meadows, verdant hills and appreciating the fertility and beauty of the Commonwealth of Massachusetts along the Indian Path, they resolved to remain in mid-western Massachusetts in a place called Quabbin, which means "land of many waters." The natural resources and the potential of attaining great wealth from the area were most captivating. They decided to settle on the shores of a lovely lake, and called it Wolfen, after a leading family amongst the band of travelers. The lake was one of the larger ones which fed into what was to be called the Swift River. The town and lake were within easy view of three hills, eventually to be called—Soapstone, Bald and Rattlesnake—and both were near twists in the trail, which would eventually be called Greenwich Road southwest of the Indian settlement of Nichewaug.

There were remnants of Native American tribes (then called "Indians")—mostly of the Nipmuc tribes—who had lived in those hill and lake regions. These Indians had loose alliances and lived in randomly scattered villages. Their links were of kinship, fur and other trade, and common enemies. As they died out from epidemics, and wars [some allied themselves with those Indians who fought alongside King Phillip (1675-1876), and others with those "Praying Indians" who allied themselves with the English Puritans and Pilgrims], they often left behind their villages and stores and stocks of corn seed. Many of the French who came that far south from Canada, and other English (Puritan and Pilgrim), took possession of these storehouses and lands as signs from the Almighty that the land was theirs by Divine Right and by the Kings of England and France. The Lutherans, on the other hand when they arrived in the region purchased land rights from the Nipmucks in exchange for beads, wampum obtained during their stay in Boston, clothing, blankets, European plantings, and promises of future profits from Lutheran commerce. All of these exchanges and promises were duly recorded in official contracts, land sales and treaties between the Lutheran elders and the sachems of the Nipmucks.

The Lutheran settlers involved the Indians in the daily commerce and the politics of the burgeoning township of Wolfen. As time passed, Indian families sent their children to Lutheran schools, public schools as they came into being, and Wolfen College. Indian families were able to grow in wealth and education alongside the Lutherans in true democratic fashion. Many converted to Lutheranism, and some to Roman Catholicism when the Benedictine Abbey was established in Wolfen; the last of these were descendents of "Praying Indians" who were sprinkled throughout the Commonwealth of Massachusetts. By the late 1860s, the Commonwealth legislated that "Indians and people of color were citizens" of Massachusetts.

These new Lutheran settlers became farmers. This way of life consisted mostly of maintenance farming or growing and maintaining livestock for one's individual survival. As time passed this small group of pioneers developed the natural resources of the area.

As they became established and wealthy, they wanted to provide a strong academic experience for students within a spiritual context. These men made their money in lumber, building materials, livestock, and feed, seed and grain, which they transported along the compass rose, from their strategic location. Their main route was from Wolfen, along Indian paths and roads to Worcester, which became a major transportation hub for all of their goods

The merchants of Wolfen increased their wealth over time, delivering quality goods in timely fashion. A small railroad, a spur from the Boston and Albany Railroad, dubbed the "Rabbit Line" connected towns and villages and reached to Wolfen. (It was called the "Rabbit Line" because of the many stops and hops the train made between towns along the line). The railroad company to Springfield and Worcester transported goods from Wolfen. When the Blackstone Canal Company began building a canal from Worcester to Providence, Rhode Island in the 1820s and as Worcester began to grow as an industrial and communications hub, the Canal gave the products from the Wolfen merchants a forty-five mile waterway to Providence and Narragansett Bay for almost 20 years. Then the Providence & Worcester Railroad opened and took over the transportation of goods, heretofore transported by canal barges.

By the late 1920s, as the Greater Boston Metropolitan area grew, the demand for water increased so much that arrangements were made to create a reservoir in the "land of the many waters." When this occured, four towns (Enfield, Dana, Prescott and Greenwich) and villages in the area were to be inundated eventually by waters of the reservoir. It was to be located some 65 miles west of Boston and was to be called the Quabbin Reservoir. Construction of the reservoir was begun in 1927 and completed in 1939. Wolfen, on one of the outermost lakes, was spared inundation, partially because of its north easternmost geographical location, just on the edge of the planned reservoir, but also because of the wealth generated by families of Wolfen. They had attained an economic and political power in the Commonwealth, and many political decision-makers were beholden to their economic influence.

The Lutherans who came to America were diverse in the religious-political beliefs. They established separate and identifiable "synods" in Pennsylvania, New York, Michigan, Minnesota and elsewhere in the heartland of America. Conflicts among the synods centered on the basic traditions and theology of the church, on "such things as the use of the German language for worship and education or adherence to the Augsburg Confession." Liberal Lutherans wanted to worship in English, support the Sunday school movement and benevolent societies, and give up doctrines such as the real presence in the Eucharist, considered to be too "Catholic" by other Protestants."

The Wittenberg families who had established the town of Wolfen, and named the lake, were Lutherans—Blocker, Ebersberger, Grabau, Hoyt, Koch, Loehe, Miller, Muhlenberg, Schwabe, Walther, Wolfen, Worley, and others.

Wolfen in the 1950s was typical of most New England small towns . . . a 10-rod wide Main Street, through which cattle were driven to the railroad for transporting. White houses along Main Street set back from the road were identical in architecture—painted white, with white low picket fences of varying sizes and styles defining the property, some with neat stonewalls, large standing elms, oaks, maples and conifers, green lawns, columned and/or porched fronts. There was an outbuilding or two, which have served for storage from the past . . . wagons, antique cars not run for years, old tack for horses . . . and now—lawn mowers, yard furniture, yard games, and such materials used for leisure time in a small town. Most of the descendents of the first families still lived in those houses.

There was of course, the Lutheran church, St. John's on the Lake, on the same site since its founding in the early 1800s. St. John's on the Lake began as a small church, and over the years grew to predominate over the center of the town and the town green with its gazebo, which was large enough for the Wolfen Lake Town Band to give concerts. On the eastern end of Main Street, there was the neat, white church: The First Congregational Church; and on the western end, there was a small All Saints Episcopal Church. All Catholics who lived in town went to St. Gregory's Church on the grounds of the abbey, which was a little bit north and west of Main Street and on the lake.

Originally, the college was named "The Lutheran College of the Commonwealth of Massachusetts". The name John Adams College was chosen at the turn of the 20th century to attract more than just Lutherans to the college. The college became well known for its academics, faculty, students and athletics. Well-endowed, it permitted a wide variety of students from many backgrounds to study there.

Professor Greenwood was one of Adams' most well-known academics. Now, Greenwood was indeed—dead!

CHAPTER THREE

Sheriff Thomas "Tommy" W. Blocker, Jr. had been elected sheriff of Wolfen when he returned from Germany after World War II. He had been a member of the Military Police which was charged with keeping law and order in the newly created American Sector of Berlin. His father, Thomas W. Blocker, had been sheriff from the late 1930s and decided it was time to retire in 1946 when his son "Tommy" came home from the war. Tommy Blocker took the call at home from Tilly, just as he was leaving for what he thought would be another quiet day. Commencement at the college was not for another week or so, and he and Worley M. Blocker his deputy and first cousin had pretty much figured out the traffic patterns for the commencement procession. It was the same year after year; for a college that only graduated 37 or so students each year, the traffic through town was less than the tourist traffic, which increased after Memorial Day with the summer cottage crowd coming to open their cabins and camps.

The call that Greenwood was dead, had apparently not unnerved Sheriff Blocker; he had served in the fighting, then in the occupation forces in Germany and did not care much for the Germans!

Blocker arrived at Greenwood's home, saw the front door open, and entered. He surveyed the front hall—the hall between the living and dining room—and walked back to the kitchen, where he saw Greenwood sprawled halfway in and halfway out of the oven. The smell of gas had pretty much disapated, and he heard Alvin and Greta on the back porch.

Blocker went over to Greta and put his arm on her shoulder as she was weeping on the porch stairs.

"Tell me about it, Greta," said Blocker.

Greta quickly said that she had smelled gas, tried to open the kitchen door but only could get it halfway open, saw Greenwood lying there. Just then Alvin arrived, and helped her open the door. Alvin picked up the story, telling how he turned off the gas, opened the windows over the sink, stripped the wide black tape off the kitchen door, and let the house air out.

Blocker listened intently, comforted Greta, and asked Alvin:

"Did you touch anything else? Was there any sign of a struggle? A tipped over chair? Anything out of order?"

Alvin replied, "It's just as you see it, Sheriff, nothing but the windows that I opened and the tape that I stripped off."

Blocker went to the phone, picked it up, and said:

"Tilly. Call Deputy Worley and send him over to Professor Greenwood's with the camera."

"He's already on his way, Sheriff. I called him just after I reached you," she said.

"Thanks, Tilly. Oh, and call Mayor Ebersberger and President Wolfen, and tell them what has happened. Oh, and one other thing, call Doc Muhlenberg at the County Coroner's Office to pick up Professor Greenwood."

"I have already done that Sheriff, they're both coming over there, as will Doc Muhlenberg."

"Tilly, I don't know what the town would do without you. Thanks a lot," said Blocker.

Blocker hung up the phone, breathed deeply, and thought: "There's no sign of foul play. It looks like Greenwood taped the doors to keep the gas in, took out the metal shelves and put them aside, laid the tape down, and stuck his head and shoulders into the oven. But why would Greenwood do himself in?"

Worley arrived. The photographs of the death scene were taken. The Mayor and College President came by and the Sheriff briefed them. The coroner came and preliminarily decided that the death was a suicide and removed the body to the town Morgue. Worley took Greta home. Alvin continued delivering milk along the route. Tilly had intercepted a few calls from customers who called the dairy looking for their milk, and passed the calls along to Alvin. Wolfen returned to the college. Blocher got into his police car and returned to the station. The Mayor answered questions from the area press back at Town Hall. Wolfen tried to be rest again . . . however, not for long!

CHAPTER FOUR

Anthony J. "AJ" L'Alba was the Editor of the college's *John Adams Patriot*. The college community and the residents of the town called it *The Patriot*. AJ had been Editor for just one academic year, his senior year at Adams. He assembled a staff of students who were "gung ho" journalists. In that short space of time, the content of the student-run newspaper improved a hundred-fold, hence, circulation increased, ads became plentiful, and the paper received a few awards from regional radio stations and from city and town newspaper editors. AJ had one or two great news' hounds, and he himself had a nose for news.

That morning, as AJ was putting together the regular Thursday edition, Diedre "DiDi" Ebersberger, one of the paper's news' reporters came running into the *Patriot's* office. She told AJ that she had overhead Deputy Worley talking in Koch's Diner about Professor Greenwood's death. She asked him all the right questions, and wanted to "scoop" the *Wolfen Eagle*, the town's weekly paper also published on Thursday, and would AJ wait until she typed up what she had heard. AJ agreed, and left space for the article to be inserted and continued pasting up Thursday's issue of *The Patriot*.

When DiDi finished, and turned over the copy to AJ, he read it, blue-lined some of the copy, and headlined it:

"Professor gassed in his own oven!"
By Diedre "DiDi" Ebersberger with Anthony "AJ" L'Alba

John Adams College, Wolfen, Massachusetts, May 5, 1955—Professor Richard K. Greenwood, popular professor of history at John Adams College, dead this morning, found by his housekeeper Greta Worley and diary owner Alvin Grabau. Professor Greenwood was found with his head and shoulders resting in his gas oven in the kitchen of his town home; the gas jets were turned on, and the kitchen was sealed with black tape. Deputy Sheriff Worley M. Blocker, who was reluctant to talk about the death, told this reporter, "that it looked like suicide, but the Sheriff has not received the Coroner's report yet." When President of Adams College, Charles B. Wolfen was asked about Greenwood's death, the President said, "I will have a statement to read to the student body later today." The Mayor wanted to talk with the Editor of the Eagle first.

The President hired Professor Greenwood at the end of World War II. Little is known of Greenwood's background, other than he was a refugee of World War II who came from Wittenberg, Germany, where he was an instructor at the University of Wittenberg. Funeral arrangements have not been made when this article was written.

AJ and DiDi looked over the copy, slotted it in the upper right hand section of the first page, and inserted a photo of Greenwood, which had been posted in an edition of the *The Patriot* when he was first appointed, and began running off the four-page issue of the *The Patriot*. Everyone associated with the paper was called in by AJ, and all distributed the paper at the usual drop off points on campus and in town. They had indeed "scooped" the local *Eagle*.

A on Friday, the "Eagle" (delayed until the story of Greenwood's death could be written) published a similar story, with the exception of naming those who were called or were present on the morning of Greenwood's death at his home. By this time, however, it was yesterday's news.

When AJ looked at the final story as it appeared in the *Patriot*, he prided himself at the headline. What he did not realize at the time was that the banner was to become one headline that would haunt him for years to come.

CHAPTER FIVE

AJ and Di-Di talked about Greenwood's death on the morning of the tragedy, and during their final weeks as student news hounds on the *Patriot*. Somehow, their inquiring minds were not put at rest by the decision of the coroner—that Greenwood's death was a suicide. There was no evidence that Greenwood was depressed; there was no suicide note? AJ and Di-Di wanted to get as much information gathered from those who were present, those who were called and those who had gathered at professor Greenwood's home on the fateful morning. Perhaps in finding out more about those who were on or about the scene, the pieces would fall into place and allay their unrest. They decided that they would put together a dossier of the people who were at the scene of Greenwood's death; and by talking to six people each would find out more about the death.

The people AJ and DiDi selected were Greta Worley, Alvin Grabau, Tommy Blocker, Worley Blocker, Tilly Loehe, Gustav Ebersberger, Josef Koch, Kurt Muhlenberg, Rolf Hoyt, George Mueller, Edward Schwabe and C.B. Wolfen—all of whom in one way or the other, were attendant upon Greenwood's death.

After having lunch together at Koch's diner, they listened to the townspeople talk about the events of the fateful morning. The comments were as diverse as the people who were expressing them. Two older women were overheard saying that Greta was "sweet on the professor." A few of the employees of the police department expressed amazement on how swiftly the coroner had decided upon a verdict of suicide. "You'd think he wanted it over and done with, and the body buried by sundown," said town hall clerk. There was no question that the town was a-buzz about Greenwood's death; the talk only reinforced AJ and DiDi's doubts.

Having agreed to interview as many people who were directly or indirectly involved after Greenwood died—townspeople who might know what happened at Wolfen Manse, AJ hoped to publish one last issue of the *Patriot* at graduation time, which would be his, and DiDi's last publishing venture. The *Patriot* was published once more with only a few inches devoted to the Greenwood death . . . . just an obituary.

But AJ was able to publish only the brief obit—a broadside was run off on the mimeograph machine in the *Patriot's* office.

> **Richard Kurt Greenwood, 33**
>
> **Wolfen Lake, Massachusetts, May 25, 1955—Richard Kurt Greenwood, 33, of Wolfen Manse at John Adams College, Wolfen, Massachusetts, on May 25, 1955.**
>
> **Born in Wittenberg, Germany in 1922, the only son of the late Lukas Maxmilian Greenwood and Marie Anna (Schaumkessel) Greenwood, had lived in Wolfen for 9 years.**
>
> **Dr. Greenwood had been a college professor at John Adams College since 1947 as a teaching professor of history.**
>
> **Until coming to America in 1947, he had been a university instructor at Wittenberg University during the Second World War, and completed his doctoral studies in history just after the war. During that time, he also worked as a translator for the United States Army in the Wittenberg region, and on the strength of that service for the military government in Germany, was able to come to America. He was appointed to the position of instructor, and within a short time became a tenured professor at John Adams.**
>
> **Dr. Greenwood was cremated and his ashes were dispersed over Wolfen Lake.**

CHAPTER SIX

AJ and Di-Di immediately set out to the task of interviewing some of the town's leading citizens about their knowledge and involvement in the aftermath of Professor Greenwood's death. They hoped to have a follow up story ready before *The Eagle* could publish its own follow up.

Di-Di found out about Greta Worely quite quickly. Greta Worley kept house for Professor Greenwood. She would come in two or three times a week to clean, do his laundry, tidy up, and would cook for him on the days that she came to the house. Greta would come to Greenwood's house on Mondays, Wednesdays and Fridays. She was faithful to her job. Greenwood paid her well for these services, so that she did not have to work for anyone else. This was a good job for her . . . . as good as any house cleaner could command. On the day of Greenwood's death, she was not scheduled to be at the professor's house. Because she could not be there earlier in the week, she postponed her work until that Thursday.

Greta's family was among the leading families in Wolfen; her family had been among those who came by wagon to Wolfen. The Wolfens ran the feed, seed and grain company in town. The Wolfen Feed and Machine Company was still run by Wolfens. Greta was the oldest in this current generation of Wolfens, and as such should have been able to become one of the managers of the store. She did very well in school, and was enrolled in the College when she developed a debilitating illness; she spent much time in hospitals and sanitariums. A bright woman, who was often seen in the town or college library reading and borrowing books, she was not able to take the stress of running a business, although she had an income share of it. She worked for Greenwood to give her something to do during the days, and she enjoyed the intellectual interchange when he was on the premises. She was always described as a "handsome woman who had some 'troubles'."

DiDi found it difficult to talk with Greta; she was suffering the effects of the loss of her friend. "When I found him, I could only say over and over, 'the professor was dead'. She repeated the phrases. "I thought I knew him better than I did. I didn't know what he had in him." DiDi, thought, "One who commits suicide often is unaware of the people left behind who cannot fathom the act. It was wrong for him to have committed suicide."

Greta continued, "We talked a lot about events in the news, the history of Wittenberg, what is was like there. You know, my own ancestors came from Wittenberg and settled here in Wolfen?"

Greta was well read, on current affairs, and was an intellectual challenge to Greenwood. She enjoyed discussing events of day with him. Some in town thought that she might have a romantic interest in Greenwood, but there was never any evidence to that effect.

"I picked up his mail at the Post Office, I cleaned for him, I sometimes cooked for him, and we talked about many things. I guess you never really get to know someone—what he was capable of doing," Greta said.

For some time after Greenwood's death, Greta was depressed, out of sorts, and quite fidgety amongst her kin. She no longer had access to Greenwood who would have known about her interests. After DiDi chatted with AJ about what she found out, AJ thought that Greta knew more than she had reported, but he could not quite put his finger on it.

Greta deteriorated over the year following Greenwood's death, and at the time of her death in May of 1956, she was in a distraught state babbling, "He died! He died! He died." She was buried in the family plot of St. John's on the Lake graveyard following a memorial service in the church.

CHAPTER SEVEN

AJ decided to talk to Alvin Grabau, who was the owner of Grabau Dairy, a full service dairy, incorporated in the Commonwealth of Massachusetts in the early 1900s. He was delivering milk on the day of Greenwood's death. The Grabau Dairy was a family-owned business providing quality products and service, of which Alvin was the President. Their products could be found in refrigerators and retail outlets in the tri-state area of Massachusetts, Vermont and New Hampshire.

He called upon Alvin at the main dairy. (Alvin was delivering milk on the morning that Greenwood died for one of his milkmen who had called in from out-of-town, and who was staying with his wife at the out-of-town home of her parents.) Alvin was a "hands-on" kind of owner. He had taken over the family dairy, which had been producing dairy products since his ancestors arrived with the first wave of Lutherans who founded Wolfen. The Grabau family owned many acres of farmland on which milk-producing cows grazed. It was the only dairy in the area. The Grabaus were known as quality producers of milk, butter, ice cream, bacon, and a variety of cheeses made from their own herds of cows and goats, and pens of pigs. The Grabau family also owned chicken farms, from which eggs were produced. Alvin's family had become quite wealthy and influential in the greater Wolfen area.

Alvin was a "take-charge" owner of the Grabau Dairy and whenever one of his milkmen was unable to make deliveries, Alvin or one of his family was called in to substitute. He took over the route that morning for John Hofstadter, a milkman who had been called out of town on the previous night to respond to a call about an illness in his wife's family who lived in Williamstown in the northwest corner of the Commonwealth. The milkman and his wife arrived at his wife's parents' home in Williamstown rather late. They found out that no one was ill, nor did anyone call from her home. Because of the lateness of the hour, they decided to stay the night; the milkman called Alvin, who understood the situation, and agreed to do his route that next morning.

AJ and Di-Di were not able to fathom how Hofstadter and his wife were called out of town for no apparent reason, or who called them; perhaps Alvin could shed some light on this minor mystery.

Alvin was a short, wiry man, who seemed to be always dressed in his light green tailored "jump suit," with his dairy's emblem embroidered on the left pocket of his outfit. He and sheriff Blocker had their outfits designed and tailored in a Newbury Street tailors in Boston. (A Grabau was a tailor there). He wore a baseball cap to match. He was not particularly a handsome man, but was attractive in many ways. He was exuberant, with crinkles at the corners of his eyes. His face was ruddy, with an omnipresent smile. In contrast to his well-designed outfit, Alvin wore U.S. Army surplus boots, which were always covered with the slurry from his pastoral lands.

He frequently wore leatherwork gloves, the fingers cut down to the palms of his hands. He needed to have his fingers "at the ready" in the event one of his cows was reluctant to give milk through his modern milking machines. At several of his dairy locations, "home made" ice cream was produced and customers could come, buy his ice creams at retail, and enjoy sundaes, frappes, ice cream floats, and other sundries. Cows would be brought in, milked by modern machines behind huge glass windows, while the public, especially children, who would come with their on families or school outings, could watch the cows being milked.

Alvin told AJ that he arrived that morning, and found Greta crying over the body of Greenwood. "She was just repeating over and over that Greenwood was dead," he said. "I got her out of there real quick. The smell of gas was overwhelming so I covered my nose, went into the kitchen to shut off gas; I also opened the doors and some windows so there would not be an explosion, and called Tilly to get the Sheriff. Although I was somewhat upset, I managed to get Greta out to the porch. She was inconsolable."

Alvin could or would not continue, he seemed shaken, and asked that AJ leave. "I'm sorry AJ, I cannot go on with this, I am so upset," said Alvin. So, AJ bid his goodbyes.

As he left, AJ was uncertain as to who might have shut off the gas. Was it Greta, who was jabbering over the body? How could she have remained in a gas-filled room without attempting to shut the jets? Did Alvin shut off the jets? Did he arrive at the same time as Greta? Too many answered questions. Why had he been delivering on his employee's route that morning? Why hadn't his milkman found anything amiss at the family home in western Massachusetts?

Alvin became blind over the next few years. The best ophthalmologists could not determine a cause. He died from an apparent heart attack in the late 1950s; he was found early one morning sitting in his favorite chair, with a copy of the Lutheran family bible in his lap opened to the passage: Judges 16:28—"Then Samson called to the LORD, saying, 'O Lord GOD, remember me, I pray! Strengthen me, I pray, just this once, O God that I may with one blow take vengeance on the Philistines for my two eyes'!"

Grabau was also buried in the family plot in the St John's of the Lake graveyard following a memorial service in the church.

AJ/s questions for Alvin went unanswered.

CHAPTER EIGHT

Tommy Blocker was a good sheriff. DiDi knew that, because she would talk to him about college students who would get in trouble with the town's police. Blocker and his deputies kept the town secure.

Blocker was a big man of over 6 feet tall. He was bulk personified. He looked like a sheriff of a small town. His dark blue uniform was not an off-the-rack model from some police supply company, but custom-made by the same tailor as Grabau in Boston. His light blond hair, slightly, but prematurely gray, gave him the look of a trusted police officer.

Working with the small college campus security department, very few major incidents requiring police intervention took place in Wolfen. The incidents were mostly of disturbance of the peace, when the college students celebrated after successful athletic events, some speeding and driving under the influence, fights in town at the local eating and drinking establishments, and when students were in high spirits during "Freshmen Week," "The Fall Festival," "The Winter Carnival," and "The Spring Fling." During these times, some drinking also took place, but it was kept mostly private, and there was the town's share of students who were drunk and disorderly. The town jail had few cells and when someone was put in a cell, it was seldom locked. Tommy was a soft-spoken, quiet town sheriff, who liked to negotiate with offenders, rather than arrest and detain them.

The Blocker family was among the original settlers of Wolfen. As time passed, and the needs of the community changed, Blocher established the first street lights in town. They also arranged water deliveries from a town well, which they had dug, owned and maintained. Eventually, they became the owners of the Blocher Gas, Light, Water and Sewer Company, and as towns were being lit up by electricity, the family became the suppliers of electricity. Their company name was Blocher Utilities.

Tommy Blocker was slated to follow in the family footsteps in moving up in Blocher Utilities; however, because of his military service, he was appointed sheriff.

When he returned from the war, he married his childhood sweetheart, and she had given him three children, two girls and a boy. Lisle was a good wife and mother and was very active in the local Lutheran church, St. John's on the Lake.

DiDi spoke to Blocker following Greenwood's death, and it was his opinion that Greenwood "did himself in," even though there was little evidence of depression prior to his death, or that anything was troubling him. His testimony at the hearing by the town fathers was a major factor in a decision by the sitting council of "death by suicide".

Blocker told the Town Council of his arrival at Greenwood's, reported the taped doors and windows, excepting the one over the kitchen sink, the gas open gas jets had been turned on (but turned off by Alvin Grabau), and the placement of the body. He said that there were no "marks or bruises on the body" and that there was only a glass with remnants of a sedative in it. He surmised that Greenwood took the sedative so that he would be asleep while the seeping gas asphyxiated him. The Coroner supported this account.

When asked by AJ, Blocker replied: "AJ, I've told all that I know to the Town Council. You heard it all. There is nothing more to say. It was a tragedy."

AJ got very little else from Blocker.

AJ had taken European and other history courses from Greenwood, and found him to be sure of himself, proud to have escaped Germany, proud to have helped the American Army with the translation of prisoner of war interrogations, and could not imagine a man so sure of himself as someone given to suicide. After all, he came through World War II, and all of its horrors, seemingly unscathed.

Yet, something continued to nag at AJ. Were there Greenwood's fingerprints on the glass? Could someone else have administered the sedative? Was the window, which was not taped, the way in which a potential murderer could have exited the kitchen? Did Greenwood know the murderer, and let her or him into his home?

Blocher died of a heart attack while on duty at the Sheriff's office one Saturday night; he was interred in the graveyard of St. John's on the Lake church following a memorial service in the mid-1960s.

———————•———————

Interlude 1

AJ and Di Di needed some time to themselves to mull over what they had learned from each of those from the Walden town who were somehow connected to Professor Greenwood's death. They needed to get away from town. They decided to commune with themselves and nature. Where best to do this but in their beloved woods and forests along Wolfen Lake. In the past, as they were growing up, they would leave their everyday world and go off together for daytrips into the wilds. These trips were an adventure, hiking trips in which they had become experienced hikers and overnighters. They knew how to travel light, yet with the appropriate things to efficiently pack and bring with them; together they learned about wild plants and their medicinal and edible uses, they found and ate wild foods and made nourishing and sustaining teas, with what they found. They had learned how to identify wild plants—which ones were edible and which were poisonous, They learned how to be safe in the wilderness and what they must do if they became disoriented in the woods; they learned how to be comfortable sleeping in the great out of doors. They kept journals and created commentary about what they had experienced and enjoyed. In sum, they were experienced in the out-of-doors.

They shook the town and the college from their feet and early one sunny spring-like Saturday morning, they packed their gear, and dressed for a good morning's hike to one of their favorite locations on the lake . . . some two hours from the town. Along the way, they traded information about what they had learned and tried to make some sense of it all.

When they arrived at one of their favorite spots about mid-day, they were able to look out over the still water of Lake Wolfen and they rested awhile.

As AJ emerged from his short reverie, he thought aloud: "Why is it that they were all called to the professor's home by President Wolfen? Why did they all have to be there?

Why was the verdict of 'suicide' given so quickly, without even an autopsy? Was the evidence so clear that no autopsy was necessary? Could something have been covered up?"

Di-Di awoke from her short nap, and responded: "AJ what did you say, I dozed off." AJ repeated his thoughts and after a moment's reflection, DI Di said, "AJ, what could they have hidden? We heard what they had to say when we interviewed them. They are upstanding leaders of Wolfen—why would they have cause to hide something?

AJ, mused: "Hmm! I don't know, something is rolling around at the back of my brain? I think we're missing something."

DiDi went on, "perhaps they all wanted to be together to see what had occurred so there would be no error in the judgment of the Doc's medical post-mortem."

"Ah," said AJ, "That must be it! The Doc wanted endorsement of his diagnosis, and the others were there to give it to him?"

"But why," AJ queried? "Why?"

Famished from the hike and from being out doors, they made a campfire and sought out their cooking gear, which they had stashed on previous trips in a natural out cropping of rock. The cast iron pot was blackened by many years of use over an open fires . . . and the melamine plastic bowls and plates were where they were left on a previous trip. A bottle of soapy dishwashing fluid had become hardened since its last use.

The took all of these down to the lake, added liquid to the soap, and put the utensils in the cold lake water . . . they scrubbed and cleaned, and the cooking and eating ware were ready for use. They built a fire in a pit, which had to be cleared of winter's debris; added some rocks from the surrounding area, found kindling and larger wood to make their fire. AJ and DiDi each had small axes with which to shorten the larger logs. AJ took out his steel and flint, and breathed fire into the kindling. Soon, having stacked the larger pieces of wood in a tepee-like structure, a campfire of sufficient proportion was eating at the wood. They had planned to make a mulligatawny soup—they boiled the water from the lake and laid in the ingredients . . . chopped onions, celery, carrots, a soup base, and some dried beef.

As the soup cooked away, they rested each on their own gathered pine bows, taking in the sounds and smells of the woods. After they had lunched, cleaned up, put away their eating tools in the covered rock, covered the fire with loose dirt, they headed back for town, arriving at dusk.

They had talked enough, and were satisfied that they needed to continue their inquiries with the townspeople.

CHAPTER NINE

Worley Blocker, the sheriff's deputy, was Tommy's nephew. Since the town was so closely knit, and many in town were first or second cousins, there was never any mention of nepotism. Worley did a good job, and was always at Tommy's disposal. Worley had attended Adams for two years, and was not doing well academicallyl but athletically, he had been the "star" quarterback on the football team. He maintained his athletic ways by running and working out at the college gymnasium, and regularly swam "laps" in the college Olympic-sized pool. He was good with numbers and arithmetic; however, he still was not able to maintain passing grades in his other courses. The football fans were upset when during the summer of what would have been his junior year, while working as a substitute clerk in the Sheriff's office, he decided to drop out of college and to continue with the Sheriff, eventually becoming a trusted deputy.

Worley married Alvin Grabau's daughter, Emma, with whom he had been dating, and on his days off from the Sheriff's department, he earned "walking around" money, doing the dairy's books. He often would substitute, as the other Grabau's did, driving the milk runs when someone called in sick or had family issues to settle.

Worley was quite casual about the death when he spoke with AJ. He seemed to take the death in stride, and did not question the verdict of suicide at the inquest.

AJ's doubts persisted. What else did Worley know? Was he purposely casual to divert AJ from the real cause of death?

Worley told AJ, "AJ, I don't know what I can tell you. Greenwood committed suicide, and that's it!" Did Blocker know more than he was telling?

Blocker died while rescuing a young child from a burning house next door to his own home in the nighttime. All the family, including their Golden Retriever, escaped. The child was on an upper floor at the window screaming; she would not jump into the waiting arms of her father. Blocker came over in his pajamas, bolted through the front door, got to the child's bedroom, and was able to drop the child to her father. Before he could get out himself, the floor collapsed, and Blocker was consumed in the flames.

Worley was buried in the family plot in the St. John's on the Lake graveyard.

CHAPTER TEN

Tilly Loehe was the town telephone operator and had been since the 1930s, when she took over the job at the local telephone company from her mother Agnes who was called "Aggie." A large woman who was given over to nibbling bon bons, pastries and soft drinks during her days on the switchboard, she wore brightly flowered dresses and stood out at church on Sunday mornings. As she was growing up, she helped her mother at the board. Tilly found a few young women from the college who were in their junior or senior years to help. She had a special, secret switch installed at the switchboard, so a loud buzzer would greet any listening-in on the phone calls. She was able to shut off and switch on at will. The push and pull system was installed at her home, so she and Aggie could monitor the switchboard twenty-four hours a day. For a while when Tilly began taking over from Aggie, those on the phone system called her "Grit," because she sounded so like her mother. Tilly knew everyone in town by voice. The College had its own internal system, and she was only familiar with those who called on outside lines, as well as the phone operators for the College. As for the pay phones in the dormitories and in other public buildings, it took her a while to recognize the voices of the many callers who used the pay phones in any given academic year. In time, as phone customers grew, and when the New England Telephone & Telegraph (NET&T) company finally came to town, the Loehe home telephone company was acquired and modernized by NET&T.

Tilly also knew the household gossip of everyone in town, and depending on where the call was going to or coming from, she often listened in when she was not very busy. She was able to alert Sheriff Blocher or his deputy about what criminal activity was being planned, who was calling while drunk, and especially during the war, she had an inside track on most of the information about those in the Army, Air Corps, Navy and Marines, such as who was killed in action, wounded and/or missing in action.

Di-Di talked with Tilly at her home at lunch in the kitchen, when a substitute operator from John Adams came in for two hours. Tilly told Di-Di, that when she got the call, she immediately recognized Alvin Grabau's voice and knew something was wrong at Greenwood's house. She followed through on everything that was asked of her, and kept in touch during the morning, until the coroner took the professor's body away.

Tilly had not been monitoring the switchboard earlier that morning; an operator from the college was at the board. Tilly had been hanging clothes out on the back clothesline, just before the call came from Alvin.

Di-Di asked, "Is there anything else you remember, or want to tell me, Tilly?"

Tilly thought for a moment and responded, "No, I don't think so, Di-Di."

DiDi had the feeling that there was something else Tilly was not telling her, but could not quite get at what it was. She knew Tilly well, and it seemed that Tilly was guarding her words as she spoke with DiDi.

Tilly died in the late 1950s while listening in on a conversation between the new pastor of St. John's on the Lake and his wife, about when she and the children would join him at Wolfen Lake. Tilly could override her own buzzer system. This was known, because the pastor testified at the inquest that Tilly began to gasp on the phone as she passed on, "I'm sorry; I'm sorry; I'm sorry!" Tilly's memorial service was well attended; she was buried in the family plot in St. John's on the Lake graveyard.

CHAPTER ELEVEN

DiDi's dad, Gustav Ebersberger, was Mayor of the town of Wolfen. The Ebersberger family was descended from the original group of settlers of the town. The Ebersbergers had harvested and grown trees in the surrounding forest; they were successful loggers, saw millers and lumberers. The Eisenbergers were well known and respected in the forestry industry in all of New England. They were among the first who initiated management planning for the industry—that management made for cleaner water, and enhanced wildlife—while maintaining profitability. They were among the earliest environmentalists, and their example of responsible forestry became a model for maintaining all subsequent New England forest ecosystems. The Eisenbergers were among the first who recommended the establishment of the U. S. Forestry Service (USFS) in the late 1800s; it was eventually established in 1905 to protect the national forests and grasslands. There were many such lands incorporated into the USFS adjoining the vast forest and grassland holdings of the Eisenbergers.

When President Wolfen called the Mayor at home, he immediately contacted his administrative assistant, to keep him informed of what was transpiring amongst the members of the police department on that day. He had planned to come to his town hall office early, but instead went to meet Wolfen at the Wolfen Manse.

DiDi had a close relationship with her dad. DiDi's mother died when DiDi was only four years old. She had been raised by her Aunt Martha (her dad's sister) who had lived with them. DiDi had hoped to speak with her father at dinner that evening, but her father seemed distracted and distraught. He usually enjoyed eating pot roast with all the fixings, but he had not really touched his food. He left the dinner table early and went over to the Eisenberger lumber office, where he stayed all evening. She never did get to talk with him on that day. Whenever the subject came up, he would become distant and evasive about what he knew about the death of Greenwood. DiDi would never find out much from her dad.

Eisenberger died while saying grace before meals at his home on Thanksgiving Day in the early 1960s. A large turnout of politicos attended the memorial service at St. St. John's on the Lake—the two U.S. Senators, several congressmen, the governor and other state officers, mayors, ex-mayors, representatives of the lumber industry, and the like—were in attendance; it was one of the largest turnouts of mourners for a town citizen that Wolfen Lake had seen in years. St. John's on the Lake was bursting at the seams.

Eisenberger was buried in the family plot in the church graveyard.

DiDi was quite saddened by her father's death; she was the one responsible for making the funeral arrangements; she was comforted in her grief by AJ, who helped her with the arrangements. DiDi and AJ went on one of their walks through the woods, along familiar paths, skirting the lake, watching the sun set, as DiDi tried to absorb the idea that her father was dead and was all alone at home. AJ assured her that she would never be alone, since he, her life-long friend, would be there for her. A few weeks after the memorial service, AJ proposed that they go see the Boston Symphony Orchestra play in Symphony Hall, have a late dinner, and return to Wolfen Lake in a hired car. DiDi welcomed the opportunity. She was able to talk with AJ on the return trip about her Dad, and how distant he was to her. She had continued to live in the family home, after her graduation from Adams; she returned there at vacation times from her graduate studies at Radcliff and Harvard. The housekeeper of many years kept the house in readiness. DiDi did not want for money, since she inherited quite a lot of money and property from her Dad; trustees at the local bank managed her finances. DiDi took her Ph.D. in Literature from Harvard in the early 1960s. and then she returned to the Eisenberger family home when she was given an instructor appointment at Adams.

CHAPTER TWELVE

Josef Koch, and the Koch family before him, owned world-famous, Wolfen Lake Hotel and Resort. The hotel was a five-star hotel and had a four diamond formal dining room; the hotel's parquet floored ballroom could hold any major festivity from the surrounding area. It boasted an indoor/outdoor pool, and an excellent spa. It was one of the oldest resort hotels in the area; it attracted lodgers and visitors from all over the northeast. The resort's advertisements were placed in all the travel magazines and the travel sections of national and regional newspapers' travel sections. From time-to-time, stories were written about "pristine acreage on the shores of Lake Wolfen . . . peaceful lodging, lake sunsets and fireside dining." The complex also offered housekeeping log cabins in pine groves along the lake. Koch's Diner, connected to the hotel, offered hearty fare from 4:30 am until 11:00 pm; it was the gathering place and hub for all the townspeople. Anything spoken about there, resounded 'round the town in no time.

Josef Koch was descended from the early settlers of Wolfen. When it was evident that the rich natural resources of the area could be developed, Franz Koch, who was with original trekkers along the Mohawk Trail, decided that he should build a rooming house cum dining room for itinerant travelers. Previously they baked bread, and pastries and Franz women-folk created colorful quilts and coverlets, and made blankets. These were sold in an annex to the rooming house. As the town grew, so did the rooming house—what finally emerged on the site overlooking the lake on the main street was an all-season inn and spa. The bakery, quilts, coverlets, and blankets, became well known and sought after by all who came to the town. To this day Wolfen Quilts and Coverlets are known worldwide. The hotel was not on as large a scale as the Mt. Washington Hotel and Resort at Bretton Woods, or the Equinox in Manchester Village, Vermont, but large and special enough to attract some of the wealthier families from the Northeast. Prominent Lutheran families made their annual summer visits, and it became an annual pilgrimage. Route 32 (which eventually became 32A) in Massachusetts was one of the more scenic routes to Wolfen Lake; coming from the south, one would have to travel through the town of Gilbertville, where there was a well-photographed, covered bridge.

AJ called upon Koch during the early hours of that fateful day. Koch was a small, distinguished looking innkeeper as befitted his station. He would personally greet families who would come to his family's hotel. He wore glasses, but would always appear with his reading spectacles, which he would put on and take off to emphasize what he was saying. AJ found him in his office which adjoined the diner. AJ had written copy for the Wolfen Lake Hotel and Spa, and Koch was pleased that AJ had called. Koch shifted some papers on his desk, looking for some ideas which he had jotted down for the upcoming summer season, and would AJ look them over and work them into flyer, which would be sent out to former guests and area newspapers. AJ took the material, promised to have something back to him in a few days, and broached the Greenwood matter.

"Mr. Koch, this morning, everyone in the diner was abuzz with Professor Greenwood's death. Who brought the news?"

Koch looked blank, and said, "Perhaps it was Sheriff Blocker who mentioned it to me; he came in for his usual coffee and donut, and told me. There were others around who may have heard him telling me. You know how those things go. A word here, a word there, and it was all over the diner."

AJ asked again, "Why would Sheriff Blocker have been so casual about Greenwood's death; we still don't know that much about it?"

Koch responded rather testily, "How would I know what the Sheriff would or would not do or say? Go write what you have to write for the paper! I've got things to do!" He abruptly left his office, with AJ still sitting there. AJ was taken aback. Koch was not usually that way. There was something that Koch knew and was not about to tell AJ . . . and left, so as not to blurt it out.

AJ did return to the college newspaper office and with DiDi together the special edition, which scooped the Wolfen weekly paper.

Koch died of old age at 95. All of his vital organs shut down after surgery for a gangrenous gall bladder. The operation was a success, but Koch's body could not take the shock. He died in the late 1990s, and was buried in the family plot in the St. John's on the Lake graveyard following a memorial service.

CHAPTER THIRTEEN

D oc Kurt Muhlenberg was the archtype for the country doctor. In his office he was always seen wearing his medical whites provided by a linen supply company from Worcester. He was a graduate of John Adams and went to Boston University School of Medicine in Boston. He learned from the best doctors in the Hub; he spent the long hours of internship and residency in Boston's gritty hospital—Boston City Hospital. After his residency, he returned to Wolfen to join his father, Franz Muhlenberg in his village practice. When his father died in the early 1950s, Doc Muhlenberg took charge of his father's patients. Doctor Muhlenberg, the elder, was medical examiner for Wolfen; shortly after his father's death, the Doc was appointed medical examiner for the town and the area. When needed, he also served as the coroner for the town.

Doc Muhlenberg knew internal medicine. He had special study and training which focused on prevention and treatment of disease. He knew how to prevent, diagnose and treat diseases. He also knew when to refer cases beyond his ability to the nearby Worcester medical specialist community. He knew about the maintenance of wellness before it became a rallying cry for the medical community; he was a good country Doc.

DiDi's father was friendly with the Doc and her family had been patients of the Muhlenbergs over the years, so it fell to her to chat with him about Greenwood's death.

They met in his office. DiDi asked him, "Doc, why do you believe that Greenwood committed suicide, even though there was no prior indication that he was 'suicidal' or depressed?"

Doc responded, "He took the trouble to tape up all the windows and doors to keep in the gas before he turned it on and lay with his head in the gas oven. Also, I did not see any evidence that he had any bruises on his body, or that he was placed there against his will."

"You know, DiDi," he continued, "Professor Greenwood was well liked at John Adams, and who would have wanted to kill him?"

DiDi mused, "Perhaps someone from his past in Germany who was jealous of him came to see him, and 'done him in'?"

"I don't think so," said the Doc. "There was no evidence that anyone was at the house before he lay down in the oven."

"Now if you don't mind, DiDi, I have to see my patients; perhaps we can talk about this at another time?"

DiDi left, but felt that the Doc was brusque with her and not being honest. She thought that the Doc knew something else, but was not telling her.

Doc Muhlenberg died in the mid-1960s while en route to a house call; he was driving his 1948 Ford "woody" on a rain-slicked highway out of town, slid on a flooded part of the road, hydroplaned, and smashed into a tree. He was buried in the graveyard of St. John's on the Lake in the family plot after a memorial service.

CHAPTER FOURTEEN

Rolf Hoyt was another descendent of the original settlers of Wolfen. His family had been amongst those early family farmers who realized that there would be need for additional goods and services for these and other farmers to come. The Hoyts established the first farm products company in Wolfen. "Hoyt's Feed and Grain Store" became the distribution point for all farming needs and products . . . as farmers themselves, they knew that they needed to create, produce and provide feed, seed, grain, fertilizer and other farm-related implements, wagons and working animals. As time passed, and as farming evolved, the Hoyts were at the cusp of evolutionary change, which came in the farming industry.

By the 1950s, Hoyt's feed and grain store had evolved into a collective of grain, feed and all related commercial interests—*Hoyt Feed and Grain, Inc.* Their stores were located in most farm communities in the tri-state area (Massachusetts, Vermont and New Hampshire).

Rolf was a graduate of the University of Massachusetts at Amherst in its agriculture program. As a land-grant university, the University of Massachusetts, Amherst was the logical choice for Hoyt; it was nearby and made it possible for him to learn agriculture at a university while still working in the Hoyt industries. The Hoyts had contributed heavily to the University's agricultural program endowment.

Rolf had become friendly with Greenwood because of their common interest in their Wittenberg ancestry. Rolf also had a strong interest in his Lutheran heritage, and often traveled to Germany and to Wittenberg. When in Wittenberg, he would visit the Castle and All Saints Church in that city, on the door of which Martin Luther in 1517 nailed his 95 theses opposing the granting of indulgences, and in which Luther's grave is found.

AJ had become friendly with various members of the Hoyt family when he worked for his father on the grounds of St. Gregory's Abbey. Although Rolf was but a few years his senior, AJ got to know him when Rolf would make deliveries of Hoyt products to the Buildings and Grounds storage facilities on the abbey grounds. They often chatted about landscaping, gardening and farming. The abbey had a small "working farm" to provide flowers, and fruits and vegetables for consumption by the monks.

AJ called upon Hoyt to ask about his friend, Professor Greenwood. Their chat was brief.

AJ first asked, "Did you suspect that Professor Greenwood might have been depressed over something?"

Rolf responded, "He didn't seem to be any different than what he was like ordinarily. Although I sensed that there was something that he wasn't telling me, during our last visit."

AJ asked again, "In my classes with him, I didn't detect that he was depressed over anything; in fact, he was his normal and usual arrogant self. Are you pretty sure that there was nothing seriously bothering Greenwood?"

Rolf said, "No. If you will excuse me, I am expecting a shipment of farm machinery, and I want to make sure that I have all the paperwork, invoices and checks."

It seemed to AJ that Rolf was like all of his other contacts after Greenwood's death, Hoyt was not forthcoming with what he knew and dismissive in his responses. He learned nothing of Greenwood's disposition before Hoyt's unexpected death in early 1960.

Hoyt was buried in the church graveyard of St. John's on the Lake in the family plot following a memorial service.

CHAPTER FIFTEEN

George Mueller was an undertaker. The family Mueller had been burying and cremating townspeople and others from the area since Wolfen Lake was settled. The mission for the business, developed through the years and emboldened on bronze plaque in the entryway to the Mueller Funeral Home was: ***The Mueller Funeral Home is an independent family run business and whether one chooses burial or cremation for your loved ones, the Mueller family will take care of all arrangements to ensure that the funeral is carried out in accordance with the wishes of the family.*** George himself removed Greenwood's body from the Manse to the morgue.

AJ met with Mueller at the funeral home late on the day of Greenwood's death, after his body had been delivered to the coroner's office. Mueller, a tall distinguished looking gentleman, was arranging for funerals and burials of at least two clients when AJ sat with him in his office. He was distracted by a several phone calls—the obit writer at the newspaper, two different cemetery managers, the representatives of the families of the deceased, and calling upon his various drivers to pick up the dead.

With one family member, Mueller said, "Funeral arrangements for your loved one are a very personal choice and our personal care will enable you to say your own farewell in the manner you choose." AJ thought that it was something that Mueller said to all who called to bury their dead. It was a statement which AJ heard many times over the ensuing years from other funeral directors. The statement was delivered in a soft, monotone; in a way, it sounded almost creepy to him. AJ, realizing that this distraction might interfere with the brief interview he had planned with Mueller, offered to come back at around 6:00 pm. Mueller was insistent that they complete the interview.

"Did you notice anything unusual about Greenwood's death," AJ asked?

"Yes. He was in his under shorts and was lying with his head in the oven when I arrived." CB Wolfen called, and I went to pick up the body. Greenwood is now at the coroner's clinic," Mueller responded. He continued, "After the coroner completes his report, at the instructions of CB Wolfen, the body will be cremated here; a simple tin urn in which the ashes were to be dispersed over Lake Wolfen at the instruction of CB Wolfen," he said again.

AJ followed up with, "I mean "unusual" beyond how you found him . . . marks on his body, unordinary bruises . . . stuff like that?

"No. It was a straightforward death. Well, if you can call lying face down in an oven, straightforward. No marks . . . no bruises . . . nothing out of the ordinary," Mueller said.

He went on without so much as a pause, "Now if you will excuse me, I have to arrange for two wakes and funerals for tomorrow. I still have not called the church. The Reverend Schwabe will have to call in another minister from Worcester to help him out with the services."

AJ said his goodbyes and thank-yous, and was leaving Mueller, just as the phone rang again. He heard Mueller say, "I'll be with you in a minute, Doc. The L'Alba boy is just leaving." Mueller looked up, and called to him, "Goodbye AJ." As AJ walked out on the porch of the funeral home, he still was sure that after a few interviews, he still believed that something other than what was told to him was not being said.

Mueller died following the funeral of Mayor Eisenberger. They said it was a heart attack. His son who had helped his dad took over the funeral home and the arrangements. It was one of the grander funerals that town had ever seen. All mourners were driven from the Mueller funeral home to St. John's on the Lake in various limousines loaned for the occasion from the various funeral homes in the area. He was buried in the family plot in the St. John's on the Lake graveyard.

CHAPTER SIXTEEN

AJ had chosen to interview the Reverend Kurt Schwabe. Schwabe as a young curate, was at a liberal Lutheran parish in another area. Once during the early 1950s, St. Luke's inspired the more liberal parishes in the Synod, but angered the more conservative—when Kurt Schwabe's wife, Christiana took a more visible role in assisting her husband in administering the church. She did the accounts, made the deposits, often appeared at services in cassock and surplus, and read some of the prayers in the liturgy. She and Kurt reached out to all ages—children, younger and older families, as well as the seniors of the parish. Christiana also worked tirelessly to interact with community social service agencies. It was when she proposed forming a council of all of the churches in the area, to work together on religious understanding, that Kurt was asked to move on to a church in a inner city. In fact, they expedited the move for husband and wife to be relocated to a Boston parish. Schwabe and Christiana were recruited by the Wolfen church wardens.

St. John's was a white clapboard church located in Wolfen; one could see the spire of St. John's on the Lake, (later changed to St. Martin's) from all approaches to the town, from miles around. Many artifacts inside the church were brought over from Wittenberg. A hanging tapestry, reputed to be one of Martin Luther's favorites, was given to the St. John's on the Lake parishioners by the parishioners of All Saints Church in Wittenberg. A wooden cross which was crafted by German woodcarvers, and which hung in one of the churches in Wittenberg, was prominently displayed over the main altar of St. John's on the Lake. Other artifacts, of museum quality, all received from the Fatherland as gifts by the St. John's on the Lake congregation were to be found throughout the church: icons, sacred vessels, paintings, altar panels, plaques.

The most significant artifact was a stole reportedly worn by Martin Luther himself; this stole was draped over a table and folded as if it was about to be worn. When it was first received, it was easily accessible to the visiting pilgrims; but over time it became threadbare and frayed. One of the Schwabes, encased the stole behind a plate glass wall when the local stores began using the new glass product. The plate glass had to be replaced several times as visitors continued to place and rub their hands on the glass in awe of the stole.

St. John's on the Lake was well known amongst the American Lutheran community as one of the oldest Lutheran churches in New England that a regular stream of pilgrims came to visit and pray.

When AJ went to interview the Reverend Schwabe he found him kneeling in prayer in the darkened church in the nave towards the rear. Schwabe was really kneeling, not bent over while sitting in the pew, as is frequently the case in some churches. His head was in his hands, and he was quietly either intoning prayers or moaning low. In the pew beside Schwabe, AJ saw "the book" from which Schwabe often quoted in Latin in class[4]. AJ came upon him quietly; it took a few moments for Schwabe to realize that he was not alone. He slowly raised his head, in the darkness; AJ could just about see his face.

The Reverend Schwabe was an adjunct professor at John Adams; he taught a course in world religions and a course in biblical themes and values. AJ had taken both courses and was known to Schwabe.

Schwabe spoke first, "AJ, I didn't hear you coming up on me."

---

[4]   The well-worn book was: *Disputatio pro Declaratione Virtutis Indulgentiarum,* by Dr. Martin Luther, 1483-1546. From *D. Martin Luther's Werke: Kritische Gesammtausgabe.* I Band (Weimar: Hermann Boehlau, 1883). Rev. Schwabe took this book to class with him often, and quoted liberally from it.

AJ responded, "I hope that I didn't frighten you, Father Schwabe?" (AJ used the greeting that he used with his own Roman Catholic priests; he could not bring himself to call a Lutheran priest, 'Reverend'.)

"I heard that you were around gathering information for the *Patriot*. How can I be of help," said Schwabe?

"You were called by C. B. to come to minister to Greenwood—to give him Extreme Unction—I guess you don't call it that, do you," said AJ.

"We at St. John's on the Lake follow the Augsburg Diet rules for sacraments. We therefore administer three sacraments, Baptism, the Lord's Supper or Communion, and absolution or penance. If the person is alive and communicative, we can administer absolution or penance, it he so desires. Greenwood was dead. I could only say a few prayers and trust that in his last moments, he was contritional. But I covered that in class once—you may have remembered," said Schwabe?

"Yes. I do remember. Then why did CB call you? Was Professor Greenwood still alive; was he a member of this congregation" said AJ?

"I came and said some prayers and hoped that he was in the frame of mind to meet God," said Schwabe.

With that, Schwabe began crying aloud. He put his head in his hands again. He left the pew and went running towards the altar. As he ran, he cried out, "Oh my God. Oh my God. Deliver me from this anguish."

AJ was surprised. Was Reverend Schwabe truly upset about Greenwood's death? Was there something else that he knew but did not tell him? The college community and the town were upset about the death of Professor Greenwood—and he supposed that many came to Schwabe in their grief.

After Greenwood's death Schwabe seemed to have lost interest in being a pastor, asked for his release, and left town; he was quickly replaced as pastor. Word came to one of the elders of St. John's on the Lake, which Schwabe had worked at Our Savior's Lutheran Church in the shadow of Logan Airport in Boston and was killed when trying to break up a fight on the street outside the mission. Schwabe's body was returned to St. John's on the Lake for a memorial service, and he was buried in the family plot in the graveyard.

The nagging continued. Later, when AJ and DiDi met at the *Patriot's* office, they both conferred about what they had found out from the various townspeople They were both convinced that there was more to Professor Greenwood's death than was told them. There were still many questions unanswered.

CHAPTER SEVENTEEN

AJ and DiDi had visited with the townspeople who were directly or indirectly involved in the aftermath of Professor Greenwood's death. Upon conferring with each other, they concluded they knew only the basic facts—that Professor Greenwood was found in his shorts with his head in the kitchen stove; the windows and doors were taped and sealed, except for a window over the sink; he was found by Greta Worley and Alvin Grabau; they proceeded to inform others in town, who came to the Wolfen Manse and performed their respective chores. The undertaker took Greenwood to the town morgue, where an autopsy was taking place to confirm death by suicide. Greenwood's ashes were to be thrown into Lake Wolfen. There would be some service at St. John's on the Lake performed by Reverend Schwabe. There might be some mention of Greenwood at the commencement exercises at John Adams College.

Other than these basics, AJ and DiDi had little to do but to write a short broadside obit for distribution at the usual places.

Was this the end of the story about Greenwood's death? AJ and DiDi hoped not, but it was to be—short obit, short story, end of story!

It was not until many years later when the entire story was told; and, C. B. Wolfen himself told it.

CHAPTER EIGHTEEN

Charles B. "Chuck" Wolfen, Jr. was appointed President of John Adams, when his father CB retired in the late 1970s. CB was named as Professor Emeritus at that time. Wolfen was to be given an honorary degree at the dinner at which others who were also to be honored at the coming Commencement ceremonies.

AJ and DiDi arrived in timely fashion and immediately began to schmooze with the invited honorees and other notables who were having cocktails, wine and hors d'oeuvres before dinner. Much of the faculty was invited and present. As is the custom at many colleges, not all faculty are invited to the dinner for the honorees; only those who have an academic interest or have been designated to accompany the honorees during their investiture. Many of the leading members of the Wolfen Lake community were also invited. It was the academic social event of the season.

Many friends and sycophants surrounded Professor Emeritus C. B. Wolfen; he was relishing the attention. He was flushed with happiness and sweating profusely. At one point, he asked for some water, saying that he felt faint. He was led to a high-backed chair in the quieter library, sat down and he began to experience pain along his left arm and radiating to his heart. He knew the symptoms. He had long been aware of the problems with his heart, and he had medication which he could press under his tongue. He reached into his pocket for that medication, found it in a small vial, and did press it under his tongue. He began to pass out and asked that AJ L'Alba be brought to him.

AJ came to him, and CB asked that the library be cleared, but that his physician should be called. Sheriff Gustav "Gus" Blocher decided to call the EMT unit at the fire department, as well.

They were now alone. CB asked that AJ to sit next to him, since he had something to say to him. AJ brought his head close to CB's face to listen.

CB began. "Kurt Greenwood was executed in 1955!" AJ gasped, but realized that the lingering story of Professor Greenwood's death was about to be told.

He continued, "Richard Kurt Greenwood lied about his credentials. The United States Army recommended him to me, since he worked as a translator for the government after the war. Although he began as a university graduate reading literature in at the at Wittenberg in 1943, he joined the SS and became Grupenfuhrer Richard Kurt Greenwood of the SS. He was in charge of leading many Germans who resisted the Nazis and Jews into the gas chambers of Sachsenhausen Concentration Camp," responded CB. "He desecrated the name of Wittenberg and of the Lutheran families who aided the Jews and was responsible for the killing of thousands of Jewish people. Thousands were executed there or died from starvation, disease and medical experiments." CB's breathing became more labored.

"How did you find out, CB," asked AJ?

"By accident, actually." Greta was cleaning the house as was her practice and came across a newly published book about the Nazi concentration camps, which she had brought in with the mail earlier in the day. She thumbed through it, and saw a photograph of young Greenwood at the Sachsenhausen Concentration Camp in Berlin. There was a caption underneath with the name: Grupenfuhrer Richard Kurt Grünes Holz!" CB was breathing and talking in such a low voice, that AJ had to press his ear to CB's lips.

The EMT unit arrived, along with the EMT technicians; his doctor was not in town, but the resident at the Wolfen Hospital would be there when he arrived. CB asked AJ to come with him in the rescue vehicle. He wanted to tell him more. One of the EMT technicians wanted to put an oxygen mask over his mouth and nose, but CB waved it off—he wanted to tell AJ more. The EMT technician was able to insert a nostril oxygen tube.

As they traveled to the hospital, CB asked the EMT technician to ride up front. The EMT woman refused, saying that CB's health and safety were to be monitored by her very closely. CB was persistent and eventually the EMT technician moved to the front. AJ continued to sit by him.

As they approached the hospital emergency room, CB motioned to AJ to come closer; CB whispered, "that isn't all there is. There's more. You will find all you need to know in your library. On the top shelf on the right, the shelf closest to the library door, there is a large green book entitled, *The Quabbin Reservoir: a History*. It is wedged in and cannot be easily moved. The center of the book is hollowed out. Inside the book is what you will want to read."

"AJ, Greenwood was evil," CB, continued, "he was responsible for terrible crimes of horror against Jews and fellow Germans who harbored Jews. For those evils, which he committed, the descendents of the Lutherans of Wittenberg, acting as a jury of twelve just and true people, did what *we* had to do."

"At the last, when *we* confronted him in what is now your home, he was not repentant."

AJ calmly asked, "Who is 'we' CB?"

CB continued, "The twelve of us!"

"The twelve of you," queried AJ?

"Now that they are all dead, and I am the last, I believe the time has come to make a clean breast of it all," he said. CB slowly and haltingly named the twelve: "Greta Worley, Alvin Grabau, Tommy Blocker, Worley Blocker, Tilly Loehe, Gustav Ebersberger, Josef Koch, Kurt Muhlenberg, Rolf Hoyt, George Mueller, Edward Schwabe, and me. We were all descendents of the original families who founded Wolfen."

"Greta brought the book to me. When Greenwood was out of the house we found other evidence in the house. After reviewing all the evidence, and, especially a trove more secretly hidden in one of the bookcases. I called them all together at my office, gave them the information, and we decided that he had to be brought to justice. So, as jury of German-Americans acting on behalf of the Lutherans of Wittenberg and Wolfen, we went about the task of his trial and execution."

CB continued. "We all went to Greenwood's home on the evening before he was "found," we confronted him with all the evidence we had. He did not repent or deny the evidence; in fact, he was proud of what he did in the Third Reich. In fact, he still held on to that sense of mission from his youth, which had been subverted by Adolf Hitler. We stripped him down to his underwear as he would have done to the prisoners he led to the gas chambers. We held him until he was quieted by Doc's injection of a sedative; we gave him a glass of water, and he spit up in it. We taped up the windows, doors and other openings with the exception of that window over the sink, through which we exited. I was the last one out, and was chosen by the twelve to turn on the gas jets. It was only right that he die by the gas oven in the John Adams college's own home—he had ordered the same for thousands in his concentration camp."

"Before he died, Greenwood took credit for his part in purifying 'the Master Race'—as he said in German—'Heil Hitler. Leben lang das Vorlagenrennen' . . . Heil Hitler—long live the Master Race'. Greenwood ended by sloganizing with Libensraum'!" (A major Nazi ideological principle, aiming to provide extra space for the growth of the German population, for a Greater Germany).

With those last words, CB took his last breath, AJ called to the EMT technician, his throat rattled, and the EMT woman got out the electric paddles to shock CB's heart into action. "Clear," she yelled. She did this several times, but to no avail. CB was dead before they reached the hospital.

AJ finally had most of the pieces of the story of Greenwood's death that had been puzzling him since his senior year at John Adams.

EPILOGUE

AJ was given a ride to his home by one of his students who worked as a ward aide at the hospital. DiDi was there waiting for him. They would all gather again the next morning at baccalaureate services at the Campus Chapel. The Board of Trustees had hastily met, having heard of CB's death, and decided that in addition to the usual baccalaureate program, the service would be a Memorial to President CB Wolfen. CB's funeral would be held a few days after the commencement ceremonies.

AJ told his long-time friend DiDi what had been told to him by the dying CB. DiDi was at first shocked, but eventually came around to the reality of it all. Together, they agreed that all that could be publicly known and written about Greenwood's death had been written. They pledged to each other not to divulge any of what CB told AJ about the justice meted out by the twelve leading citizens of Wolfen, all of whom were now dead. No justice could be further obtained by exposing these newly discovered facts.

AJ and DiDi went to the library in his home, found the book, *The Quabbin Reservoir: A History*, and with some effort, took it from its resting place of many years.

Behind the book, there was a lever; AJ pulled the lever, and the bookcase quietly slid open. The open bookcase revealed another set of shelves on which there were many mementos of the SS and Nazi era. The top three shelves behind glass windows, held a collection of Allach porcelain—vases, bowls, small statues representing a wide variety of images held dear by the Nazi faithful. AJ remembered that this porcelain, as fine as an Oriental, English or French pieces, were crafted by the inmates of the concentration camps. These pieces were only made for top members of the Nazi party and the SS. The collection was a beautiful array of porcelain, but a gruesome reminder of the events of the holocaust. On other shelves were reminders of the Nazi party: Daggers with leather handles emblazoned with the SS symbol were laying there. Several pistols and hand weapons were among the collection. Calipers used to measure head sizes and to determine "Perfect Aryans" were placed in a velvet-line jewelry box. There was also a Magnetofon—a tape recorder, with a tape on its reels. AJ and DiDi did not move any of these items. However, they would return to the early made-in-Germany magnetofon.

They then turned their attention to the book. Before opening the book, AJ and DiDi put on a pair of latex gloves, so as not to leave their fingerprints upon the contents. In the hollowed out section they found: a leather booklet with the SS symbol on the cover, and the names of all SS members who had fled Germany (photographs, original names and assumed names, and amounts of money given by Holz) ; a black book which included numbered Swiss Bank accounts, listing amounts, dates and payouts to various SS members; a roll of microfilm in a metal case—later found to include photos and identifying marks of an entire grouping of SS officers; and, the Iron Cross, and other medals inscribed to "Ricard Kurt Grünes Holz." Kurt was a member of Leibstandarte SS Adolph Hitler, the Fuehrer's private army and death squad, which killed scored of rival Nazis in a 1934 purge known as the "Nacht der Langen Messer" (Night of the Long Knives). The Germans to this day call the event the "Rohm-Putsch" to describe the murders associated with Ernst Rohm, the leader of the Sturmabteilung, which was getting out of hand. Not only was Greenwood in the SS, he was a one of a group of principal contacts for ex-Nazi SS officers who had made their way to him for payments from large Swiss Bank accounts.

AJ and DiDi, put the book aside, and took down the Magnetophon. It was a small battery operated unit, of very lo-fi, which the German army members used in the field for interrogation purposes. [German radio had higher fidelity units, which they used for broadcast purposes. They were the primary developers of the magnetic tape recorder. All Allied countries' radio broadcasters, manufacturers and recording engineers were on the look out for this electronic development from 1944 to 1946, when the war was winding down and after the war had ended. Many soldiers in the field picked them up at radio stations run by the Germans; they disassembled them, mailed them to the U.S., where they were re-assembled]. As they did so, they saw neatly packaged tapes with German writing in red grease pencil, stacked behind the tape recorder. The battery on the Magnetophon was long dead. Later on, with the help of the audiovisual chief at the college, who was able to determine the voltage, a direct current adaptor was fashioned to the Magnetophon. The tape that was on the machine, and cued up halfway through, was of the cries of agony of the victims of Nazi brutality, crying out in various languages and dialects, mostly in Yiddish, about the unspeakable atrocities which were heaped upon them. Greenwood must have taped and re-lived those events in the privacy of his college home. The other tapes were similar, a veritable cache of recorded horror.

AJ and DiDi were aware of the SS, and were horrified that they were now seeing the aftermath of the SS's existence in Germany. They knew of course that the SS was originally established by Hitler in 1925 as an section of the SA for political purposes—to protect speakers at public meetings of the Nazi Party. (SS—"Die Schutzstaffeln der Nationalsocialistischen Deutschen Arbeiterpartei" was part of SA—Die Sturmabteilungen der Nationalsozialistischen Deutschen Arbeiterpartei.)

When the Nazis had obtained power, the SS was used to preserve order and manage audiences at mass demonstrations. The SS was given the duty of "internal security" by decree of the Fuehrer. The SS performed a vital function at the time of the Roehm purge of the 30th June, 1934. As a prize for its services, it was made an independent unit of the

Nazi Party. From that time until the end of World War II, the SS brought to trial at Nuremberg, the SS committed "crimes against peace, war crimes and crimes against humanity."

All night long, they poured over the material, and were able to understand the extent to which Greenwood was a key player in the escape route for ex-Nazi SS officers.

Eventually, on a trip to Boston, AJ was able to mail a packet, which included everything found in the hollowed out section of the book to the Boston FBI. He also sent the cache of tapes. The FBI never did a follow up which led AJ and DiDi to assume that they knew about Greenwood all the time[5]. AJ, and with the help of DiDi and her family's financial contribution, dedicated a small section of the college library, as a museum to the victims of the holocaust. The Allach porcelain, as was the Magnetophon, was placed on permanent display, along with other holocaust items given by alumni and parents.

For AJ and DiDi, this discovery sealed their pledge not to divulge the mystery surrounding Greenwood's death. They cracked open AJ's favorite bottle of vintage port, Quinta do Vezuvio produced in the 19th century, sipped it from cut lead Spiegelau crystal liqueur glasses and watched the sun rise over the college campus.

The professor was indeed dead, and justice was served by a jury of his German—American peers—now all deceased! Or, was it?

—The End—

---

[5]   The FBI knew of many former Nazi party members who were relocated in secrecy to the USA after the war. Often, their identities were buried in the vaults of the FBI. These members proved to be helpful as informers to the FBI and other USA national security interests. Eventually, many were found out, and brought to justice. The Wolfen community was among the first to mete out justice to a Nazi war criminal.

ADDENDA: HOW AJ D'ALBA BECAME A CARDINAL AND WHY

POPE ANDREW ABDICATES!

Notes about Pope Andrew and the sequence of events to elect the next Pope.

Pope Andrew, among the youngest of Popes of the Roman Catholic Church, became the first Bishop of Rome in six centuries to abdicate from office as of Ash Wednesday. Andrew was suffering from an incurable illness, which was never specified to the public . . . the illness, drained him of his strength, and his ability to strongly lead the Church. AJ and some few others in the Curia knew that he had an inoperable tumor in his brain, which was slowly draining him of strength, vision and thought.

While such papal abdications are extremely rare, there are precedents in the two millennia history of the Catholic Church.

Marcellinus: This early church pope abdicated or was deposed in 304 after complying with the Roman emperor's order to offer sacrifice to the pagan gods.

Benedict IX: Sold the papacy to his godfather Gregory VI and abdicated in 1045.

Celestine V: Overwhelmed by the demands of the office, this hermetic pontiff stepped down after five months as pope in 1294. Pope Benedict XVI prayed at his tomb in the central Italian city of L'Aquila in 2009.

Gregory XII: The last pope to abdicate, Gregory XII stepped down in 1415 to help end a church schism.

U.S. Catholic Church prelate, the Cardinal Archbishop of New York looked at the legacy of the Pope: what he leaves behind; who is most likely to succeed him; and what to expect in the coming days and weeks as the Church prepares for the papal transition.

The Pope's announcement eases the way for a successor who will confront the task of rebuilding the church's foundations in an increasingly secular world while continuing to spread its roots in the rapidly growing emerging nations.

The 50-year-old Pope, who before his election was Cardinal Aldo Ciminiano of Rome.

The abdication of Andrew, heads a church of one billion plus Roman Catholics worldwide.

Pope Andrew is considered by many to be a leading theologian, a deeply spiritual leader, and a charismatic speaker/preacher.

The last pope to abdicate was Pope Gregory XII, who stepped down in 1415 to end a dispute among those who were claiming the Chair of Peter.

As in every era, there are obvious front-runners. The cardinals are now expected to meet in early March for the conclave, the secret meeting to elect a new pope.

There's no consensus around a single prelate of the Church, except Cardinal Manfredo Ernesto di Toscano, the Cardinal Archbishop of Milano, Italy, who already has a following of Cardinals throughout the world who are seeking doctrinal changes; as a block, they are will to revisit doctrines already addressed and decided upon by Councils of the Church, among them: Bogomils in modern day Bosnia, a sort of sanctuary between Eastern and Western Christianities. By the 11th century, more organized groups such as the Patarini, the Dulcinians, the Waldensians and the Cathars were beginning to appear in the towns and cities of Northern Italy, Southern France and Flanders; and, Arianism, concerning the Divinity of Jesus Christ.

Sequence of events to elect the new Pope

The Camerlengo or Chamberlain will steer the Cardinals to make Conclave plans to elect a new Pope. He ensures that the Papal apartments are locked and sealed; he also sees to the destruction of Andrew's Papal ring.

When there is no Pope, this inter regnum, is known as "sede vacante" or "vacant see"—the transition from the end of one Papal era to the beginning of another. A period of some 20 days will occur and will be overseen by a few in the Vatican who will be guiding the College of Cardinals in their deliberations. Those who will be guiding this transition are:

- Cardinal Francesco Malozzi who is the Camerlengo will be responsible for guiding the Holy See. He will take possession of the Apostolic Palace and "safeguard and administer the goods and temporal rights of the Holy See."
- Cardinal Bartolomeo Pescadoro, who is the Dean of the College of Cardinals, he is responsible to officially summon the Cardinals to the Vatican to participate in the Conclave.
- Monsignor Giuseppe Stefano Brunetti is the Master of Liturgical Ceremonies is responsible to conduct the religious elements of the Conclave and the Mass of Installation of the new Pope. He will be present when the Dean asks the newly elected Pope if he accepts the election.

- *The Dean of the College of Cardinals, Cardinal Francesco di Parma, will lead the con-celebration of the "Pro eligendo Pontificie" Mass (the Mass for the Election of a Pope) inside St. Peter's Basilica.*

- *Upon the completion of the Mass, lunch is served and the Cardinals retire to the Pauline Chapel; they, then process into the Sistine Chapel intoning the Litany of the Saints . . . they call upon the Holy Spirit in Gregorian Chant to intervene in their deliberations, take their oath of secrecy of Conclave proceedings, which will be followed by a meditation by an elderly Cardinal, Cardinal Robert von Weber. By the time they reached the Sistine Chapel, they will sing, invoking the Holy Spirit, "Veni, Creator Spiritus".*

- *The master of papal liturgical ceremonies announces the order, "Extra omnes" ("Everyone out")—all, excepting the taking part in the Conclave leave the Sistine Chapel. The doors to the Sistine Chapel are closed and the Vatican's Swiss Guards stand guard in front of the doors, as the Cardinals begin their deliberations*

- *The Cardinals also vowed that if they were elected Pope, they would faithfully fulfill the ministry of universal pastor of the Church and would defend the rights and freedom of the Holy See. They solemnly swore to follow the rules for the election of a Pope and keep secret the results of the votes, unless they have express permission from the new Pope to reveal details. Each Cardinal walked up to the Book of the Gospels, put is right hand on it, said his name and sealed his oath, "Sic me Deus adiuvet et haec Sancta Dei Evangelia, quae manu mea tango." ("So help me God and these holy Gospels that I touch with my hand")*

- *According to that which was pre-agreed, at informal meetings held by the Cardinals, each Cardinal was provided a few minutes each to introduce themselves before the voting began.*

- *As the voting takes place, each Cardinal writes his choice on a rectangular piece of paper inscribed: "Eligo in summen pontificem" ("I elect as Supreme Pontiff"). After writing the name of his Choice, each Cardinal places it in a bowl intoning, "I call as my witness, Christ the Lord, who will be my judge that my vote is given to the one who, before God, I think should be elected."*

- *After the vote, and counted by three Cardinals, re-counted by three Cardinals, announced, and pinned together through the word "Eligo," the ballots are placed in the cast iron stove installed especially for the purpose of ballot-burning, and burned with special chemicals. Black smoke means that a new Pope has not yet been elected . . . white smoke means that a new Pope has been elected. After a short period, the newly elected Pope is led into the Sistine Chapel "Room of Tears, where his outfitted, prays alone, then proceeds to the balcony overlooking St. Peter's Square . . . .*

- *Cardinal Michael Bosworth is the Proto-Deacon who will announce to the world that a new Pope has been elected. He will announce "Habemus Papam!" ("We have a Pope") from the loggia overlooking St. Peter's Square, after the white smoke has risen from the smoke stack of the stove especially set up in the Sistine Chapel for that purpose and that purpose alone.*

Pope Andrew will be the Emeritus Pope and will be addressed as "Your Holiness." He will wear white, and will place himself under the authority of the new Pope.

The Vatican summons a Conclave of Cardinals that must begin 15 to 20 days after Andrew's abdication on Ash Wednesday. Cardinals who are eligible to vote must be under 80 years of age, are sequestered within Vatican City and take an oath of secrecy. There are 120 Cardinals under the age of 80, including A.J. Alba, whom Pope Andrew made a Cardinal in secret. The Pope gave as A.J's mission, that through all moral and legal means, the Cardinal Archbishop of Milan and his rogue Cardinal followers, should not conspire to elect Cardinal Manfredo Ernesto as the next Pope. 70 of the 120 were appointed by Pope Andrew, and none will turn 80 before the Conclave is held. Tradition has been that any baptized Catholic male is eligible to elect a Pope, but only Cardinals have been selected since 1378.

After an opening Mass attended by all Cardinals present, two ballots are held every morning and two every afternoon in the Sistine Chapel. To elect, a two-thirds majority is required. After each round of voting, the ballots are burned. Black smoke means no decision has been made. White smoke announces that the Cardinals have chosen a Pope and he has accepted. Bells also announce the election in order to help avoid possible confusion over the color of the smoke coming from the chimney of the Sistine Chapel.

The Pope is introduced from the loggia overlooking St. Peter's Square with the words, "Habemus Papam!" ("We have a Pope.") The Pope then imparts his first blessing to gathered crowd and to the world.

HOW AJ ALBA HELPED POPE ANDREW AND THE CHURCH

When AJ studied at the Pontifical North American College in Rome (Institute of Continuing Theological Education (at the suggestion of the Monks of St. Gregory's Abbey in Wolfen—who also arranged residence for him at the Abbey of Sant'Anselmo in Rome), he met and became quite friendly with a Monsignor Aldo Ciminiano who was a resident and student at the Abbey of Sant'Anselmo on the Aventine Hill. Aldo held a minor position in the Vatican. [Sant'Anselmo is not an abbey as other abbeys with a resident monastic community but it is a house of studies for monks and others who come to study in Rome].

They enjoyed each other's company. Both were theological scholars, and tested each other on various aspects of Christian theology. There were devoted to the SUMMA THEOLOGICA of St. Thomas Aquinas, and became fairly expert as a result of their dialogues. AJ attended daily mass at Sant'Anselmo, which was often said by Aldo. They often took their meals together.

When AJ returned to Wolfen Lake, he maintained a steady correspondence with Aldo, who rose quickly through the ranks of the Vatican as a theological scholar. He was named a Cardinal by the then Pope. Upon the Pope's death, at the Conclave, Aldo was elected Pope, and chose the name Pope Andrew.

When Pope Andrew assumed his Papacy, he often called upon AJ to help him with some major theological issue, and was often summoned to the Vatican by Andrew to confer with him. It was at one of these conferences, when Andrew gave him the "Red Hat" [(***In pectore*** (*Latin* for "in the breast/heart") is a term used in the *Catholic Church* to refer to appointments to the *College of Cardinals* by the *Pope* whose names are not publicly revealed (*viz.*, reserved by the Pope "in his bosom")] and charge him with keeping in touch with the conspiracy led by *Cardinal Manfredo Ernesto di Toscano.*

When Andrew abdicated, and visited the Shrine of Our Lady of Lourdes "to immerse himself in the waters," AJ was summoned to the Conclave at the Vatican. He did all that he could to influence other Cardinals to choose a Pope from one of the emerging nations, and perhaps, from South America. All of those Cardinals which he would mention were not of those Cardinals who were in Manfredo's camp. He had to do this in a short period of time, before the opening sessions of the Conclave.

At the conclusion of the opening Mass of the Conclave (the "Pro eligendo Pontificie" Mass), Manfredo was found dead in the sacristy of the Sistine Chapel, with a bottle of his family's wine, opened by his side. AJ's mission was clouded by the death of Manfredo. He was asked by the abdicated Andrew, to investigate the death. AJ called upon some of Manfredo's Cardinal followers, to shed light on his death. As he interviewed them separately, he pieced together this story (in the tradition of Miss Marple, Hercule Poirot, Dick Francis and Donna Leon:

THE BACK STORY

*W*hen Manfredo was a child, in his native Tuscany, his mother Concetta, and his father Tomaso, who was the manager of Thomaso's family vineyards (Ernesto & Son—vini di Toscano), were often in violent arguments about raising Manfredo (Concetta wanted Manfredo to be a priest, and Tomaso wanted him to follow him in managing the family vineyards). Tomaso was quite friendly with the Cardinal Archbishop of Milano, who enjoyed Tomaso amarone-like wines, and was able to secure contracts with the Archdiocese to supply all its parishes with sacramental wine. Because of the Archbishop's influence, Tomaso also obtained a contract with the Vatican for his highly prized sacramental wines. The arguments would continue over the years, until Tomaso in a fit of rage, and drunken stupor, violently attacked Concetta, and as a result, she became an invalid who had lost her hearing and speech. Manfredo had experienced these abusive episodes, and though he was closer to his mother than his father, and shared her devotion and desire to have him become a priest, he harbored a deep-seated hate for his father, and the church to which his father was doing quite well financially. They lived well in a villa, with many servants, and many workers who were in a feudal relationship with Tomaso. When Tomaso died, his younger brother Giorgio, assumed management of the vineyards. Giorgio saw to the continuing care of Concetta, until she also died.

The Archbishop took Manfredo under his wing, saw that he was properly educated, and eventually was ordained a priest whose preaching skills and gregarious nature made him a favorite amongst the priests and people of the region. He became an aide to the Archbishop, and over the years, Manfredo *also was appointed by the Pope as Archbishop of Milano. In time, and because of tradition within the Church for the Milano archdioceses, Manfredo was named a Cardinal.*

Cardinal Manfredo still harbored some deep-seated ill feelings towards the Church, and made as his personal mission to re-visit the failed schisms and heresies throughout Church history, including reversing the newly established popular tradition of taking the Body of Christ at Mass under both species and was able to influence other Cardinals similarly.

When Pope Andrew abdicated, Manfredo saw his chance. According to one of his Cardinal followers, in whom Manfredo confided (he subsequently resigned and retired to a Carthusian Monastery to repent the error of his ways), the pretender to the Papacy, commandeered a shipment of sacramental wine from his family's vineyard which was destined to be used in the Conclave. He personally injected the wines to be used at the Opening Mass of the Conclave with a high-tech poison, which would not be detected, by taste or smell.

Upon Manfredo's arrival at the Conclave he asked for his Cardinal followers to vote for him on the first ballot, and under no circumstances to take the consecrated wine when it was distributed at Mass; this would be a sign that the real presence of Christ was not in the wine. Manfredo believed that with most of the Cardinals would be fatally poisoned but that his own followers would not. He would assure his election as Pope on the first ballot. Not all of these Cardinals knew about Manfredo's plan to poison the other unsuspecting Cardinals. However, they did go along with the "no wine" suggestion, since they wanted to demonstrate their interest in undoing the option of receiving under both species.

As the Mass proceeded, and the bread and wine were consecrated to become the Body and Blood of Christ by the Cardinals who concelebrated, the Body and Blood were distributed. Some of Manfredo's Cardinals by habit, took some of the wine . . . others did not, and neither did Manfredo.

When Mass was finished and the final blessing was given by the officiating Secretary of the Vatican state, no one had died . . . no one gave evidence of being poisoned.

The Cardinals chatted and prayed as they went off to breakfast, before the casting of the two ballots.

Manfredo, very upset, went into the sacristy, found one bottle of the sacramental wine unopened, hence not consecrated, opened it, and tasted it; he immediately died!

The Conclave was temporarily postponed and the Cardinals stood down. As AJ explained to a group of Cardinals who had gathered, Manfredo had forgotten that when the wine was consecrated at Mass, the mystery of Transubstantiation has taken place.[6] The wine had indeed become the Blood of Christ, and no poison was found therein.[7]

By the time that the Conclave was to begin, Andrew had returned to the Vatican, and situated himself in an Abbey on the grounds of the Eternal City, with no intention of letting it be known other than to his private staff, that he had returned.

Since Andrew was feeling no pain after the visit to Lourdes, he summoned the Swiss oncologist (Maximilan Blenheim-Burger, MD), who examined him thoroughly, and could not find any evidence of his tumor. Astounded at his findings, he called upon a cadre of eminent Roman oncologists, to review his findings. They all concurred. Though it was too soon to proclaim Andrew's cure as a miracle, the news was known now by private staff, physicians, and others in the Roman Curia, there was a buzz

---

[6]   When a priest or Bishop consecrates the species during the Eucharistic prayers, the species is turned into the body (the bread) and blood (the wine) of Christ while retaining its form as bread and wine. In the Gospel we are told, that we must eat His flesh and drink His blood. **Transubstantiation** (in *Latin, transsubstantiatio*) is the *change of the substance* of bread and wine into the Body and Blood of *Christ* occurring in the *Eucharist* according to the teaching of some Christian Churches.

When at his *Last Supper, Jesus* said: "This is my body", what he held in his hands still had all the *appearances* of bread: these "accidents" remained unchanged. However, the Roman Catholic Church believes that, when Jesus made that declaration,[1] the *underlying reality* (the "substance") of the bread was converted to that of his body. In other words, it *actually was* his body, while all the appearances open to the senses or to scientific investigation were still those of bread, exactly as before. The Church holds that the same change of the substance of the bread and of the wine occurs at the *consecration* of the Eucharist.

[7]   ". . . they will pick up snakes in their hands and be unharmed should they drink deadly poison; they will lay their hands on the sick, who will recover.' (Mark, Chapter 16)

around the Vatican, which somehow drifted in to the Conclave. Upon hearing this news, the Cardinals, no longer in the privacy of the Conclave, called upon Andrew to address them. At breakfast, one morning, before the balloting begun, Pope Andrew addressed the Cardinals: "I have returned from Lourdes, and eminent oncologist doctors have examined me and have found me cured of my illness. I am grateful to you for your prayers and intercessions." The Cardinals erupted in calling out, "Viva la Madre di Deo," "Vivo Christe," e "Vivo!"

When the Conclave reconvened, and on the first ballot, Andrew was elected as Pope by acclamation—all ballots were cast for him! The ballots were threaded together, following their being placed by each Cardinal in one of the runs provided. As the three Cardinals tabulated the votes, it became clear that each of the ballots had been cast for Andrew. They were brought to the recently installed special ballot-burning stove, the chemicals were added to the adjoining stove, and white smoke erupted at the apex of the chimney. The crowd in St. Peter's square saw the white smoke, and were ecstatic, ebullient and overjoyed; the bells of the Vatican, Rome and whole world rang out . . . and when it was announced from the loggia "Habemus Papam!", Andrew came out to administer his blessing, and the crowd at first were awestruck, but as it sunk in, the roar of the crowd, which lasted for many minutes, could be heard rebounding throughout Rome and the world.

Lightning Source UK Ltd.
Milton Keynes UK
UKHW011109201020
371910UK00001B/32